Harry on Vacation

Also by Dyan Sheldon

Novels
Harry and Chicken
Harry the Explorer

Picture Books
I Forgot
The Whales' Song
A Witch Got on at Paddington Station

Harry on Vacation

Dyan Sheldon
illustrated by
Sue Heap

CANDLEWICK PRESS
CAMBRIDGE, MASSACHUSETTS

For Harley
D.S.

For Caz
S.H.

Text copyright © 1992 by Dyan Sheldon
Illustrations copyright © 1992 by Sue Heap

First U.S. paperback edition 1995

Library of Congress Cataloging-in-Publication Data

Sheldon, Dyan.
Harry on vacation/Dyan Sheldon ; illustrated by Sue Heap.—
1st U.S. ed.
Summary: Harry, the cat-like alien, accompanies Chicken and
her family on a camping trip.
[1. Cats — Fiction. 2. Extraterrestrial beings — Fiction.
3. Camping — Fiction. 4. Family life — Fiction.
5. Vacations — Fiction.] I. Heap, Sue, 1954 – ill. II. Title.
PZ7.S54144Haq 1993 [Fic]—dc20 92-52999
ISBN 1-56402-127-0 (hardcover)—1-56402-443-1 (paperback)

2 4 6 8 10 9 7 5 3 1

Printed in Great Britain

Candlewick Press
2067 Massachusetts Avenue
Cambridge, MA 02140

CONTENTS

A Camping We Will Go

"Think of it," my father said. "Breathing clean air. Sitting around the campfire, telling stories. Sleeping out under the stars. Really seeing the land of our ancestors." He looked around the dinner table, smiling at each of us. "This vacation will bring the past alive."

No one smiled back. My brother, Ben, was mashing his peas one by one with the back of his fork. My sister, Lucy, was staring at her plate. I was gaping at my father.

"It's going to be wonderful," my mother agreed. It was her turn to smile. "You children are growing up so quickly," she informed us. "We should do more things as a family while we can."

"Precisely," said my father. "A camping vacation is not only an excellent way of seeing the country, it'll bring us all closer together." He looked as though this should make us happy. It would never occur to my father that we didn't want to be any closer together than we already were.

I glanced at my sister and my brother. Lucy was rolling her eyes. Ben was pretending to choke.

I'm ten, my sister's fifteen, and my brother's thirteen. Ben's into playing soccer, watching other people play soccer, and seeing how much food he can stuff into his face at one time. Lucy's only interested in herself, clothes, boys, and herself. The only time either of them ever talks to me is when I've done something to annoy them. Like breathe. Sitting down to supper together is about as close as we get.

"I don't see why we can't get closer on a beach in Greece," Lucy grumbled. "I don't see why we have to do it in a moldy old tent in the woods."

"I don't see why we can't go sailing," Ben chipped in. "Why can't we see the land of our ancestors from a boat?"

I couldn't believe my parents had suddenly changed their minds about how they wanted to spend their vacation this year. For months all they'd talked about was how nice it would be not to go anywhere for a change. No rush. No crowds. No traffic. No instant coffee. It had sounded good to me.

"I don't see why we can't just stay at home," I said.

I'd already planned my summer. I was going to spend every day with Harry. Harry's my cat. Only he's not an ordinary cat. He just looks like an ordinary cat. He's really an alien visitor from the planet Arcana. Looking like a cat is his disguise. And it's a very good one. He fools everybody. He even fooled me at first.

Anyway, Harry's spaceship left him behind, and now he's staying with me until it comes back for him.

Harry's very interested in twentieth-century
life. So I'd promised him that as soon as the

summer vacation came, I would have plenty of time to show it to him. We would go for bike rides. We would go walking. We would take the bus around town. We would watch videos. We would play with Julia, our new friend who lives behind us. We were going to have the most fun ever.

My mother put down her fork with a patient, motherly sigh. "Because," said my mother.

"And don't ask 'Because why?'" said my father.

"I don't have to," said Lucy. Her voice was wobbling. She was getting ready to cry. "I know why. It's because you want to ruin my summer."

"And mine," mumbled Ben.

I said, "Mine, too."

"No, it's not," said my mother. She was still sounding patient, but not very patient. "It's because your father and I think that it would do you all a lot of good to find out about your country."

My sister rolled her eyes again. "But I know about my country, Mom," she groaned. "I have lived here for fifteen years, you know."

"Lucy's right," said Ben. "I don't want to

spend my summer having a history lesson."

"It won't be a history lesson," said my father. "It will be living history. Just think what that means."

"I know what that means," said my sister in a croaky voice. The tears started to fall. "It means we won't have any fun."

"It means I can't earn any money," said Ben. He shoved his plate away. "If I can't be on a boat, I want to save for a new bike."

"Harry and I had plans, too, you know," I told them. This news upset no one.

"John," said my mother. She was so surprised that the three of us were agreeing on something for a change that she could hardly speak.

My father folded his hands on the table. This meant that we were about to get a lecture. "It's not just that a trip like this will be educational," said my father. My father's a teacher. He likes things to be educational. "It's that it'll be different. A different kind of vacation. A vacation that involves us all." He shook his head. "You don't just want to sit on a beach all day doing nothing," said my father.

"Oh, yes, I do," sobbed Lucy.

But my father didn't hear her. "That's what's wrong with the world today," he went on. "Instead of talking to each other, people watch TV. Instead of doing things together, they lie on the beach. When I was a boy I would have given anything for a vacation like this."

"When you were a boy they probably hadn't discovered Greece yet," mumbled Lucy.

That he heard.

"Lucy," said my father. "That's enough. We're all going camping. And that's final." He rubbed his hands together. "We're going to have a great time," he said happily. "A real family vacation." He smiled. "Mark my words, this is going to be a vacation none of us will ever forget."

Aside from my mother and father, there was only one person in the family who wanted to go on this stupid vacation. That one person was Harry.

"Cheer up," said Harry. "I'm really looking forward to it. It'll be just like the old days."

"What old days?" I asked.

Harry had never visited the twentieth century

before, but he has been on planet Earth a number of times. He practically discovered it, according to him. According to Harry, he's had some incredible adventures and met some of the most famous people who ever lived. In fact, according to Harry, my family and I are the most ordinary and uninteresting humans he's ever known.

Harry gave me one of his "Oh, Chicken" looks, as though he couldn't believe I had to ask.

"The old days," he repeated. "I did quite a bit of traveling on Earth in the sixth century." He licked one paw. "I'm surprised I never told you about it."

"Well don't tell me now," I ordered. "The last thing I need now is a history lesson. I'm going to have enough of that this summer."

Harry and My Parents Have a Difference of Opinion

The fact that Harry was the one family member who wanted to go on this vacation made it sort of funny that Harry was also the one family member who wasn't allowed to go.

"I don't believe it," Harry fumed when I told him. He was standing on my dresser, knocking things over with his tail. "You're going away for *four* whole weeks? Without *me?*"

"It's not my fault," I said. "My parents have made up their minds."

"Change them," said Harry.

"I tried." I sighed. "Mom says that no one's ever heard of a cat going camping."

Harry flicked his tail. My watch fell off the

dresser. "And whom exactly did she ask?" he wanted to know. "Dog owners, maybe?"

I picked up the watch and put it out of his reach. "No, Harry," I said reasonably, "I don't think she actually went around asking people—"

Harry flicked his tail again. The keys to my bicycle lock crashed to the floor.

"Then how does she know?" he bellowed. His fur was standing straight up. He has an awful temper for a creature with superior intelligence. "She certainly didn't ask me!"

"They worry about you," I fibbed. My parents worry as much about Harry as they worry about Superman. What they worry about is how much trouble Harry causes. "My father thinks you wouldn't enjoy camping," I fibbed some more. "He thinks you'd be unhappy having to sleep on the ground. And the food's not so good, you know. No pizza or sloppy joes or anything like that."

At the mention of food, Harry's fur started to fall back into place. "That's why they don't want me to go?" he asked. "Because they're worried about me?" He's also very vain for a creature with superior intelligence.

"Uh–huh." I had my fingers crossed so hard they hurt.

The truth was that my parents said they were going on vacation to relax and enjoy themselves. There was no way they were taking Destructor Cat along to ruin it for them. Destructor Cat was my father's latest nickname for Harry.

"They know how delicate and sensitive you are," I continued. Once you start fibbing, it's very hard to stop. "They don't want anything to happen to you."

Harry gave himself a little lick. "Chicken," said Harry, "Chicken, maybe I should tell you about the time I helped the Celts fight the Saxons."

Chicken is *my* nickname. My parents gave it to me when I was little because I had a stuffed chicken I used to carry around with me everywhere. My real name is Sara Jane, but Harry never calls me that. I sat down on the bed. "The Saxons?"

"After the Romans left Britain." Harry's tail moved back and forth. "Most unpleasant people, the Saxons, if you ask me."

"*You* fought against the Saxons?"

"Yes, I did, actually," said Harry. He shuddered. "They were dirty, they were noisy, and they smelled like old boots."

I'd believed it when Harry told me that he sailed with Columbus. And I'd believed it when he told me that he went to China with Marco Polo. But Harry fighting the Saxons? That didn't sound like the Harry I knew. He didn't even like to get his paws wet.

"Harry . . ."

Harry flopped on his back. "Actually, I was very close to King Arthur," he informed me smugly.

Now I knew he was putting me on. "Who are you kidding?" I laughed. "No one's even sure that King Arthur really existed."

"Of course he existed," said Harry. He gestured with his front paws. "Can you imagine what Britain was like in the sixth century, Chicken? It was wild; wild and dangerous. They didn't have cars, you know. There were no soft beds, Chicken. There were no service areas where a fellow could get a peanut butter sandwich and a milk shake." Harry is very fond of peanut butter sandwiches and milk shakes. Peanut butter and jelly, and banana milk shakes.

"No," I said, "I don't suppose there were."

Harry stretched out on the floor. "But I survived, didn't I? As delicate and sensitive as I am." He rolled on his side. "I survived disease and bad cooking. I survived droughts and storms. I survived battles and barbarians." He twitched his ears and yawned. "Tell your parents that, Chicken," said Harry. "Tell them I'll be all right. I traveled with Arthur; I can travel with them." His eyelids were starting to droop. "Tell them they don't have to worry about me."

"But Harry," I protested. "Harry, I've tried to tell them. They won't budge. You know how stubborn they can be."

His eyes were almost shut. "Chicken," said Harry, sleepily but firmly, "you'll just have to tell them again, won't you?" He curled his tail around his feet. "You know how I hate being away from you." He started to snore.

I just stood there, looking at him for a few minutes. When it came to being stubborn, my parents had nothing on Harry.

"No," said my mother. "For the hundredth time, no. Absolutely, positively no. I don't want to hear another word about it."

"But, Mom," I argued. "Mom, Julia's mother said she'd be happy to have me. Really. She said it would be a pleasure. She said, 'Sara Jane, it would be a pleasure to have you stay with us while your family's away.'"

My mother looked up from the book she was reading: *A Traveler's Guide to Historic Places*. There were a lot of pictures of old churches in it. "Chicken," said my mother, "it's very kind of Mrs. Andreas to invite you to stay with them while we go on vacation, but the answer is still no. You're coming with us."

"But my paper route . . ."

"I thought Julia was taking over your paper route."

"But —"

My mother gave me one of her I-have-spoken looks. "No."

I knelt down beside her chair so she could see how serious I was, and how much pleasure Mrs. Andreas would have if I were allowed to stay with Julia during August. "Mom," I said. "Mom, I can't be cooped up in a car and a tent with Ben and Lucy for a month. I really can't.

Just think of what it'll be like. It'll be awful, Mom. They don't like having me around. They think I'm stupid."

"Sara Jane, really! I've never heard of anything so ridiculous. Ben and Lucy love you. You're their little sister." My mother thumped her book shut. "Where ever did you get the silly idea that they think you're stupid?"

"From them." I leaned closer to her. "They're always telling me I'm stupid, among other things. That I'm a pain in the neck. That I'm a baby. That I own the fattest, laziest cat in the universe."

My mother gave me this sort of hopeless look. "They're just teasing," she said at last. "You know they don't really mean anything by it." She patted my head. Ben and Lucy aren't the only ones who think I'm a baby. "Anyway, darling," — she smiled — "this is a family vacation. What kind of family vacation would it be without you?"

This was the moment I'd been waiting for. "But, Mom," I said slowly. "Mom, Harry's part of the family, too. What kind of family vacation will it be without Harry?"

My mother gave me another look. This one wasn't hopeless. It was annoyed. This one was her Harry look. "I should have known!" She sounded annoyed too. "I should have known that cat was behind this."

"He's not just *that* cat, Mom. He's special."

"That's right," said my mother. "He's a menace."

Imagine that you're a visitor from another planet. You don't know your way around. You're not used to the way things work in the twentieth century. You make a couple of tiny mistakes — the kind of tiny mistakes that anybody might make. Mistakes involving shopping centers, vets, dogs, and food, for instance. And what happens because of these tiny mistakes? My mother never forgives you, that's what happens. Months later, my mother's still afraid she might run into the vet on the street.

"No, Mom, he's not a menace, he's misunderstood. He's my best friend, Mom. He's my companion. My pal. Mom, I promised Harry we'd spend the whole summer together. I can't go back on my word." I was practically begging.

"Sara Jane," said my mother, "Harry is a cat. One does not make promises to a cat."

I was forbidden to mention that Harry was not a cat but an extraterrestrial. It was one of the rules my parents made me agree to before they said he could stay with us. Another rule was that I had to keep him out of trouble. It was a lot easier not to talk about his being an alien than it was to keep him out of trouble.

"We made plans, Mom. I can't desert him for four whole weeks. He'll be so bored and lonely."

My mother laughed. "Bored? Chicken, Harry

does nothing day after day but eat and sleep and eat. As long as Julia remembers to feed him every hour or two, he probably won't notice you're gone."

"Mom, please. It won't be any fun for me without Harry."

My mother folded her arms. That was a bad sign. She peered at me over her glasses. That was a worse sign. "No," said my mother. "That cat causes enough mischief when he's safe at home. There is no way we're taking him out into the unsuspecting countryside with us."

"But he'll be good, Mom." I crossed my heart. "I promise he'll be good."

"Stop being ridiculous," said my mother. "Ben didn't carry on because he can't bring Rambo and Madonna, did he?"

"But Rambo and Madonna are parakeets! Harry's practically a person."

My mother picked up her book again. Harry might be practically a person, but he wasn't practically a person that my mother liked. "I hope you're all packed, Sara Jane," said my mother. "We're leaving tomorrow at the crack of dawn."

Harry took the news very philosophically. For him. "Leave it to me," he said. "I'll think of something."

My heart sank. *I hope not*, I thought.

Harry Thinks of Something

The first thing I heard when I woke up the next morning was what sounded like someone falling down the stairs. There was a loud crash, and then my father started shouting and screaming. He was shouting so loudly that he woke Harry.

Harry raised his head from my pillow. He opened one eye. "What time is it?"

"It's six o'clock."

Harry shut his one eye. "A.M. or P.M.?"

"A.M."

His head flopped back down. "Wake me when it's daylight," he mumbled.

I gave him a shake. "Come on Harry," I

urged. "It's daylight now. We've got to get up. My dad's already packing the car."

Downstairs my father was still yelling. "Three suitcases, Marilyn? Why do you need three suitcases? We're going camping in the woods, not cruising in the Mediterranean."

At seven o'clock my father came into the kitchen, where Harry and I were having our farewell breakfast. He was smiling. "Well, Marilyn," he said to my mother, "it's pretty tight, but I've finally gotten everything into the car."

"What about the food?" asked my mother.

"Food?" asked my father.

My mother pointed to two enormous cardboard boxes, our giant cooler, and the big wicker picnic basket sitting on the floor by the stove. "I told you to put them in first," said my mother.

My father held up his hands. "Don't worry," he said. "It won't take me a minute to make a little more room."

At eight-thirty Ben came out of the front door with a huge canvas bag. I was giving Harry a good brush before I took him to Julia's, and my

mother was watering her roses.

My mother sighed. "I thought you'd already put your things in the car," she said.

"That was just my clothes," said Ben. "This is the important stuff."

"Take it to your father," she ordered. My father was still putting the food in the car. "I'm sure he can find some room for it."

At nine-thirty, because I couldn't put it off any longer, I left the house with my bag over my shoulder and Harry in my arms. My father and Ben were standing at the curb, staring into the car. They were both sweating. "I don't understand it," my father was saying. "I was sure I'd left enough room for everyone to have a seat."

My mother was standing on the lawn, shouting up at the bathroom window. "Lucy!" she was screaming. "Lucy, what are you doing in there? Come down here right now!"

"Mom," I said. "Mom, I'm taking Harry over to Julia's now." I looked at Harry. His eyes were closed and he was snoring. His chin was resting on my shoulder. I couldn't help it — I started to cry.

My mother didn't even look at me. She didn't even kiss Harry good-bye. "Come right back," she commanded. "We're going in ten minutes."

Leaving my father and brother pulling things out of the car again and my mother shouting up at Lucy, I trudged down the street. As soon as we'd turned the corner Harry woke up. "Stop here, Chicken," said Harry.

I stopped. We were in front of a low brick wall. "Here?"

"What did I say?" snapped Harry. He can be really touchy when he doesn't get his own way.

"What for? We can't keep putting it off, Harry. My parents are almost ready to go."

Harry's tail curled around my arm. "Did I ever tell you that I once worked with a very famous magician, Chicken?" he asked. "He was a truly gifted man."

I've never really cared for magic acts. Once, when my best friend Kim lived across the street, her mother hired a magician for her birthday party. He wore a turban and a red suit. The turban fell off when the paper flowers got stuck up his sleeve, and the pigeon pooped on the carpet.

"Harry," I said. "Harry, I can't listen to one of your stories now. We have to get you to Julia's." Besides, it was really hard to picture Harry sitting on a stage while a man in a turban pulled rabbits out of a hat.

Harry looked up at the sky. He went on as though I hadn't spoken. "One of his most famous tricks was the Disappearing-Cat Trick," said Harry.

"What?" Maybe this wasn't just one of Harry's stories. Maybe Harry *had* thought of something.

Harry explained the Disappearing-Cat Trick. In this trick, Harry the cat was placed in a carved gold box. Then the magician closed the box and locked it with a jeweled clasp. Then he waved his hand over the box and said the magic words. When he opened the box, Harry was gone. "It used to bring the house down," said Harry. "No one could figure out how he did it."

"How did he do it?" I asked cautiously.

Harry frowned. "Why, by magic, of course. He was a magician, you know. Not a plumber."

Sometimes I really wanted to pull his tail.

"Well, that's not a big help to us," I complained. There wasn't any time to argue about whether there was such a thing as magic or not. "I thought you'd figured out a way to come with me."

Harry jumped out of my arms and onto the wall. He shook himself. "Of course, I have seen fake magicians do that trick, too."

"Really?" I sat down beside him. His eyes stared into mine. Sometimes, like now, they were so gold they seemed to shine. "How?"

Harry smiled. "The idea is to make people believe you're doing one thing, while you're really doing something else." His smile grew. "It always helps to have two boxes," he added.

"Two boxes?"

He rubbed against me. "Or one bag."

I looked at Harry. Harry looked at me.

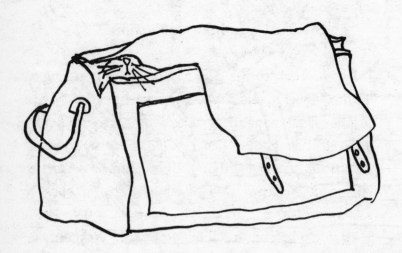

"You mean put you in my bag?" I tried not to think of what my mother was going to do to me when she found out. Somehow, I always found myself going along with Harry's ideas, even when I knew I shouldn't. "You mean only pretend to take you to Julia's?"

"Just try not to bump me around too much," said Harry. "And don't forget that I'll need some lunch."

I opened my bag and Harry climbed in. I zipped it shut, except for a small opening for air. "Now remember," I warned him, "don't move or make a sound until I tell you it's all right."

A small gray nose appeared at the opening. "Trust me, Chicken," said Harry.

"And whatever you do, don't snore."

"Me?" said Harry.

I went back to the car. My father was sitting in the driver's seat, muttering to himself. My mother was sitting in the passenger seat with her arms folded across her lap. My brother was staggering toward the house with Lucy's record player in his arms. My sister was in the back seat, crying.

"I don't believe it," Lucy sobbed. "Not only

do I have to sleep on the ground, but there isn't any electricity!"

"We're in luck, Harry," I whispered. "They're not even going to ask about you." I didn't have to pretend to be upset. Nobody was paying the least bit of attention to me. We'd be on the road in no time. Soon we'd be too far away to turn back.

I got in the car and put my bag on my lap. My feet were on a box of pots and pans, my brother's backpack was poking into my shoulder, and the armrest was jabbing into my side, but I didn't mind. The important thing was that I was in the car and Harry was with me. My heart was pounding. Where was Ben? I was afraid to breathe until we actually started moving.

Ben came running back, squeezed into the seat with me and Lucy, and slammed the door.

"Okay, Dad," said Ben. "We're ready."

"Right," said my father.

I could just see Harry's damp little nose twitching through the opening in my bag.

"Let's go," I said.

"Did you lock the garage?" asked my mother.

My father got out, marched up the driveway, and locked the garage.

He jumped back into the car. "Is everyone ready?"

"We're all ready, Dad," I told him. "Let's go!"

"Just a minute, dear," said my mother. "I'm not sure I turned off the kitchen light."

My father went back into the house to see if my mother had turned off the kitchen light.

My father got back into the car. "Okay everybody?" he asked. "Are we ready to go?"

"Okay," said Ben.

"Ready," said my mother.

I said, "Let's go."

Lucy had to go to the bathroom.

By the time she got back to the car, my father had the engine running.

"That's it!" he cried. "We're on our way!" He looked at his watch. "Twelve forty-five," he announced. "That's not too bad. We'll be able to do a little sightseeing on the way and still reach Dorset well before dark."

I hugged my bag. At last the car was beginning to move. Slowly at first, and then faster. We reached the end of the road. We turned left. We came to the first traffic light. We turned right. We were going to make it. This was going to be even easier than I'd thought. All Harry had to do was stay hidden and quiet for an hour or so and that would be it.

We were about four minutes and thirteen seconds away from our house when my mother started sniffing the air.

"What's that smell?" she asked. "Is there a

dump around here, John?"

"I can't smell anything," I said.

"Smells more like sewage," said my father.

Ben and Lucy started gagging.

"P.U.!" gasped Ben. "It smells like Godzilla farted." He started rolling up his window. Then he stopped. "That's not coming from outside," he decided. "It's coming from back here!"

"Don't be ridiculous," said my mother. "There's nothing in this car that could smell that bad."

"I can't smell a thing," I said.

"I'm going to be sick," screamed Lucy. "Pull over, Dad! I'm going to be sick!"

"Just hang on for a minute, Lucy," my father pleaded. You could tell that it had taken us so long to get going that he didn't want to stop for anything. Not even vomit. "We'll be past it soon."

"But Ben's right," moaned Lucy. "It's not coming from outside. It's coming from back here!" And then she got this look. This look of total and complete understanding. And then she went crazy. "It's that cat!" she shrieked. "I'd know that smell anywhere. It's that cat! He's

been eating cheese!"

"Chicken!" My mother turned around in her seat. She was holding her nose. "Chicken," said my mother, "where have you hidden that cat?"

My father pulled over and stopped the car. He turned to look at me, too. "Destructor Cat strikes again," he said.

Harry the Happy Camper

My father wouldn't go back.

"It's taken us over five hours just to get out of the driveway," he said. "If we turn back now, we'll be lucky to get onto the main road by the end of the week."

"But John —" said my mother.

"We're going on," said my father. "We'll be in Dorset for supper, or I'll know the reason why." He glared at me in the rearview mirror. "Sara Jane will just have to keep that cat in line. No more cheese."

"She was told that Harry couldn't come," said my mother. "And now you're saying he can." She folded up the map and stuffed it into my father's hand. "You can do your own navigating," said my mother. "I'm on strike."

My father pretended not to mind. "Lucy," he ordered, "take the map. You can navigate."

"I can't read in the car," said Lucy. "It makes me feel sick."

My father flipped the map over his shoulder. "Ben," he said, "it's up to us men."

"Aye, aye, captain," said Ben.

"And as for you, Sara Jane," said my mother, "I'm warning you. If that cat causes one bit of trouble, no matter how small, we're leaving him by the side of the road for the wolves to eat. Is that understood?"

I hugged Harry. "Yes, Mom," I answered. "We understand. Harry will be good."

Harry's stomach growled.

We drove hundreds of miles that first day.

One reason for this was that our captain refused to use the highway. "We want to *see* Britain," my father kept saying, "not just drive through it."

The other reason was that our navigator kept getting confused or falling asleep. "I can't help it," moaned Ben. "This is more boring than watching a movie with subtitles."

Every now and then my mother would look up and say, "Isn't the countryside pretty? Isn't it nice to be out of the city?"

No one would answer her, and then my father would start explaining about the Celts, the Romans, the Angles, the Saxons, or the Norsemen again. He became excited whenever he saw a hill or rock that might have been a popular meeting place for cavemen. "Marilyn!"

he'd shout. "Check the guidebook. I'm sure there was a prehistoric settlement there!"

I'd never seen so many trees, fields, or old churches before in my life. It was pretty, all right. Pretty boring.

We were lucky to reach Wiltshire in time for supper.

"This is excellent," said my father. "In fact, it's perfect. We can spend a few days exploring the area. There's a lot to see. There's Bath, there's Salisbury Cathedral, there's Salisbury Plain —"

Ben perked up. "Did you know there have been more sightings of UFOs on Salisbury Plain than anywhere else in Britain?" he asked. "I wish we had a telescope."

Harry purred in his sleep.

"Science fiction," said my father. "What we're interested in is history, not science fiction." He gestured toward the countryside. "And believe me," he went on, "there's plenty of history. Stonehenge . . . Avebury . . ."

"Didn't Stonehenge have something to do with King Arthur?" I asked.

My father laughed, shaking his head. "There is a legend that Merlin made Stonehenge as a tomb for King Arthur's uncle," he explained. "But it's only a legend, Chicken. Stonehenge has existed for thousands of years. It was originally used by prehistoric people as a burial ground."

"Hey, Dad," said Ben, "didn't the Druids sacrifice ugly young maidens at Stonehenge? Maybe we can leave Lucy and Chicken there." And he started choking with laughter.

Lucy whacked him over the head.

"What I'm interested in is supper," said my mother. "Let's find a campsite."

At the mention of supper, Harry opened his eyes.

By the time we found it, the campsite was almost full. We were lucky to get a spot right at the end, miles from the showers and practically in the middle of the woods.

Lucy refused to get out of the car.

"Forget it," she said. "I'd rather sleep in a tree for the rest of my life than spend one night in a tent with the fart factory and that spoiled brat."

Lucy didn't think it was fair that I was allowed to bring Harry along and she wasn't

allowed to go to the beach.

"Lucy," said my father, "be reasonable, will you? We have three tents. One for your mother and me, one for Ben, and one for you and your sister. If you don't sleep with Chicken, you will be in a tree."

"Why don't you put Chicken and Harry in a tree?" said Ben. "That's where they belong."

Ben didn't think it was fair, either. He said I always got my way because I was the youngest.

"Stop it, both of you," my mother ordered. She started hauling things out of the back of the car. "Lucy," said my mother, "I'm too tired to argue with you tonight. You can sleep in the car."

Lucy smiled triumphantly.

My mother started poking through boxes. "John," she said. "John, where did you put the butane for the camp stove?"

"What?" asked my father.

My mother gave him a look.

"You know," said my father, "it's really too late to cook tonight. Why don't we just have sandwiches?"

Not only would no one help me and Harry put up our tent, no one wanted us anywhere near them.

My parents said they'd had enough of us for one day, especially of me and Harry. "Just keep out of my way," said my mother. "You know I don't think that cat should have come."

Ben said Harry sounded like a herd of hippos when he snored.

"I don't want you within ten miles of me," said Ben. "I'd be happy if you camped in the next county."

"Don't put your tent anywhere near this car," warned Lucy. "If I catch one whiff of old gas-breath, I'll feed him to the wolves."

So I put up our tent in a little clearing on the other side of the path from everyone else. Harry watched.

"Ah, nature!" said Harry, leaning against my sleeping bag with a happy sigh. "Just look around you, Chicken. Look at the sky! Look at the trees! Listen to the birds! Smell the air!" He took a deep breath.

"I can't look now," I grunted. "I'm trying to get the tent up, you know." Every time I got it to stand, it fell right back down.

Harry yawned. "You don't have that pole in deep enough, Chicken. That's what you're doing wrong. Why, I remember one time with Arthur —"

I cut him off. "Harry, if I put that pole in any deeper, the tent will be so low we won't be able to *crawl* in."

Harry flicked a fly away with his tail. "Then you should put the last peg a little more to the left."

I glanced down at the illustration in the instructions. It did look as if that peg should be a little more to the left. "I knew this vacation was a big mistake," I said as I made the adjustment. "It's hardly begun and already it's a disaster."

Harry scratched his ear. "Has anyone ever told you that you complain too much, Chicken?" he asked. "I, for one, am having a delightful time." He took another deep breath. "You know, it really is nice to be out in nature, remembering how people used to live, how things used to be." He scratched his other ear. "Living history," said Harry, flopping on his side. "That's what it is. Living history. Already the memories are coming back."

Out in nature? He hadn't even walked from the car. I glared at him. Some memories were coming back to me, too. Memories of how

Harry always left me to do all the work. "It would be a lot nicer if I had some help," I said.

Harry's tail twitched. "But I have been helping you, Chicken."

I stepped back. The tent was standing.

"You see?" said Harry. "How would you have managed without my advice?"

Harry Under the Stars

We didn't sit around the campfire, telling stories, that first night. No one was really in the mood for stories. And anyway, we didn't have a campfire. The six of us just sat around the folding table, trying to keep the bugs away. My parents kept yawning. Some adventure. Lucy complained about being eaten alive and Ben went on about all the spiders, snakes, and bats there were around. Except for that, no one had much to say. Especially not to me and Harry. I think we were all relieved when it was time for bed.

As soon as we got into our tent, Harry stretched out on the air mattress. I started checking for spiders and snakes. I thought Ben might be right about them.

"What are you fussing about, Chicken?" asked Harry. "Just look at the way the moonlight falls across the trees. Isn't it lovely?"

Lovely? The moonlight? The only thing Harry usually described as lovely was pizza with extra cheese. I glanced over. "I'm looking for snakes and spiders," I told him. "I don't really like sleeping so close to the ground."

Harry wasn't listening. He tucked his front legs under his chin and gazed out at the sky. "You know," he continued, "it really is starting to come back to me. The places I've been, the sights I've seen. Your father's right, Chicken, the past is all around us."

The past was all around us? What had gotten into him? I wondered. He'd had a cold supper and he was missing his favorite TV shows. It wasn't like Harry not to complain. He had that in common with my sister. I checked our bed. No snakes under the mattress. No spiders in the blanket. I shook out my sneakers.

"I traveled a lot in this area with my magician, you know," he told me. He sighed. "What with one thing and another."

"What happened to King Arthur?" I teased. "Was he busy that week?"

"Oh, Arthur was around," Harry replied solemnly. "But I didn't really enjoy traveling with Arthur. He always insisted on going by horse." Harry shuddered. "I really can't stand horses. They're very big."

"How did this magician travel then?" I asked. "By flying carpet?"

Harry ignored me. "Actually, we had quite a few adventures, my magician and I," said Harry. He closed his eyes. "He was a man who never liked to stay in one place for long."

Pretty sure that there weren't any snakes with us, I pulled down the flap. I suddenly felt very alone in our tent. I sat beside Harry to take off my shoes. Sometimes I really like Harry's stories, but tonight all I wanted to do was go to sleep. I was hoping that when I woke up, my family wouldn't be so mad at me anymore.

"Stop making things up," I said grumpily. If it weren't for Harry, Lucy would be sleeping with me, and she could worry about the snakes. "What would a magician be doing in the middle of nowhere? There aren't any theaters around here."

Harry's eyes opened slowly. "Chicken," said Harry. He sounded bored. "Chicken, he wasn't *that* sort of magician. *My* magician did not wear a black cape and pull bunnies out of a hat."

What other kind of magician was there? "Oh, sure," I scoffed. I reached into my bag for my pajamas. "And what was your magician's name? Houdini?"

"Merlin, actually," drawled Harry. He rolled over on his side.

Merlin! First King Arthur, and then Merlin. I should have known.

"Merlin never performed cheap tricks, Chicken. The man was a master, an artist. Why, I remember the night he brought down the tents of our enemies with just a flick of his finger. You should have heard the yelling and screaming!"

I nudged him. "Harry," I said, "don't go spreading yourself out too much. I have to sleep here, too, you know." My father had said this was a two-man tent, but the two men he meant must have been Grumpy and Sneezy. The air mattress alone took up half the space. I pulled on my pajamas before anything could bite me. I wondered if I should wear my rain hat to bed. Ben said bats liked to nest in your hair while you slept.

Harry's whiskers twitched. "He could wink and turn the night into day," Harry said.

"That's nice, Harry." I unrolled the sleeping bag. With one hand I lifted Harry, and with the other I put the sleeping bag over the mattress. I turned off our flashlight and climbed in, trying not to think of snakes, bats, or spiders.

Harry kept talking. "He preferred to turn himself into a greyhound or a stag, of course — he was known for that — but those were commonplace parlor tricks compared with what he could really do —"

"I'm tired," I told him. I snuggled under the covers. "I really don't want to hear about this now."

All of a sudden, Harry sat up. "Chicken," hissed Harry. "Chicken, don't you think it's very dark in here?"

"That's because we're in the woods," I said sleepily. I didn't really want to think about how dark it was, or about how far away my parents'

tent was. "It's supposed to be dark."

"Chicken," said Harry. "Chicken, did I hear something about snakes and spiders?"

My eyes felt very heavy. "Harry, please . . ."

"Bats?" asked Harry.

"Harry, lie down!"

Harry didn't lie down. "I never had to worry about that kind of thing when I was with Merlin," said Harry. "If we came upon something disagreeable, he'd just change it into something pleasant. I remember once he turned a swarm of bees into a flock of nightingales. It was magnificent, Chicken, truly magnificent." He was almost purring. His voice began to blend with the sounds of the night outside.

My eyes closed. I felt myself drifting toward sleep. I saw stars and birds and a long road stretching ahead of me. I saw a field of collapsing tents, and Ben to one side, doubled over with laughter. I saw Lucy dancing on a beach in her pajamas, surrounded by horses and bats. Harry floated by on a flying carpet. My mother walked through the fallen tents, carrying a pot of coffee. And then, all at once, I was on a windy plain. Roman soldiers were running past me. Overhead, the lights from thousands of UFOs twinkled brightly. I could hear someone whispering, *The past is all around you . . . all around you . . . all around . . .* Then everyone disappeared. I was all alone. I started to walk. It was so dark that I could take only one tiny step at a time. And then I heard it — a horrible scream.

Yahoooooooooooooooooooooooooooooooo!

I froze.

Yahoooooooooooooooooooooooooooooooo!

It must be a ghost, I thought. A ghost from the past. "Mom!" I shouted. "Dad! Harry! Help me! Hurry!"

Yahoooooooooooooooooooooooooooooooo!

I began to run. There was an explosion of red light, and what felt like a dozen knives cut into my flesh.

Yahoooooooooooooooooooooooooooooooo!

I woke up.

"What is that?" whispered Harry. He was sitting on my chest, holding on to me with his claws.

"Let go of me, Harry!" I ordered. "That really hurts."

"Do you think we should run for it?" asked Harry. "Before it's too late?"

Run? I had a twenty-five-pound cat on top of me. I couldn't even move.

I gave him a shake. "Harry!" I was trying not to shout too loudly. The last thing I wanted was to wake my parents up. "Harry! Wake up, you're dreaming!"

"I am not dreaming," snapped Harry. He pulled in his claws, but he pressed closer. I could smell the salt and vinegar potato chips from supper on his breath. "Didn't you hear that howling?"

"It was nothing," I answered, trying to convince myself. I stroked his head. "You were having a nightmare."

His eyes glowed in the dark. He really can be touchy. "I was not having a nightmare, Chicken. I definitely heard something. Something inhuman."

"Harry —"

"Really, Chicken. There's something out there!"

With all Ben's talk, Harry was scaring me a little. I knew snakes and spiders didn't make too much noise, but I wasn't so sure about bats. "Well of course there's something out there, " I said reasonably. "We're in the woods."

"Be quiet, Chicken!" hissed Harry. "Listen! There is something there!"

I listened. From somewhere to our left I heard

an eerie moan.

Yahoooooooooooooooooooooooooooooo!
Yahoooooooooooooooooooooooooooooo!

It was the ghost from my dream. Only now I
wasn't asleep. "Maybe it's an owl," I suggested.

But even as I said that, I heard another sound, this time on our right. It was a crunching, crackling sound. The sound of something walking stealthily toward our tent.

"That's no owl," said Harry. "It has shoes on." He stuck his nose in my ear.

Crunchcracklecrunch.

Crunchcracklecrunch.

Yahooooooooooooooooooooooooooooooooo!
Yahooooooooooooooooooooooooooooooo!

I couldn't tell whose heart was beating louder, Harry's or mine.

"Your mother was joking about the wolves, wasn't she?" whispered Harry.

"Of course she was," I whispered back. "There aren't any wolves around here. And besides, wolves don't wear shoes any more than owls do."

Yahoooooooooooooooooooooooooooooooo!
Yahoooooooooooooooooooooooooooooo!

"We have to get out of here!" said Harry. "It's Merlin's enemies. They want to get even for the trick with the tents. We'll be trapped in here, Chicken. We have to get out!"

Crunchcracklecracklecrunch.

I wasn't really too wild about the idea of leaving the tent. Whatever it was, it was out there, just a few feet away. I figured we were safer inside. "Why don't we just stay here and see what happens?"

Harry's tail thumped against my head. "And be sitting targets?"

"Harry —"

"Chicken —"

Yahooooooooooooooooooooooooooooooooo! Yahooooooooooooooooooooooooooooooooo!

Crunchcrunchcrunch.

Then there was a terrible whooshing sound, and the tent came down on our heads.

I screamed. I screamed, and Harry jumped out of my arms. "Harry!" I yelled. "Harry! Where are you?"

He was trying to dig his way out of the tent. I could hear his claws scratching furiously against something. And then there was another whooshing sound, only this one was from underneath us, not above us. The air mattress collapsed and I bumped to the ground.

"Harry! What are you doing?"

"Get me out of here, Chicken!" yowled Harry.

He'd given up trying to dig his way out and was trying to tear an opening in the tent. "Get me out now!"

I grabbed hold of him and started dragging him toward what I hoped was the entrance. "Stop squirming!" Harry was making so much

noise that I couldn't hear anything else. Finally, I found the flap and we sort of fell through it, panting. Several dark, winged things sailed past our heads. Harry yowled again and leaped out of my arms. I just lay there for a few seconds, afraid to move.

And then I heard it. Loud, uncontrollable, and inhuman: the unmistakable sounds of my brother and my sister laughing themselves silly.

Suddenly a flashlight beam lit up the night. It was aimed at me. "You were right, John," said my mother. "This is going to be a vacation none of us ever forgets."

Battling in Britain

It wasn't fair. The whole thing was Ben and Lucy's fault, but did my parents blame them? No, my parents did not blame them. My parents blamed me and Harry.

"But we're the victims," I argued. "They really scared us. We didn't know what was out there."

"Ben and Lucy did not make such a racket that the entire campsite woke up," said my mother. You could tell that she didn't like getting out of bed in the middle of the night. She looked unhappy standing in the woods in her pajamas and bathrobe. "Ben and Lucy did not make a hole in your brand-new air mattress."

My father was dabbing antiseptic on his

scratches. "Ben and Lucy didn't refuse to come down from a tree for nearly an hour," said my father. He winced.

"Get your sleeping bag if it's still in one piece," said my mother. "You can spend the rest of the night with us."

I wasn't so sure about spending the rest of the night with them. I was afraid Harry might fart or something and they'd get angry again. "But—"

I shouldn't have worried. "Not *that*," said my mother, shining her flashlight on Harry. The way he was sleeping in my arms, he didn't look as though he had bones. "Destructor Cat stays outside."

"But Mom—"

My mother glared at my father.

"Chicken," said my father. "That cat has done enough damage for one day. He stays outside where he can't get into too much trouble." He laughed. "After all, these woods have been here for thousands of years. I'm sure they can withstand a night of Harry."

When I woke up the next morning, my parents

were gone and Harry was snoring beside me. I wondered how he'd gotten in. There were crumbs in his whiskers.

My parents were outside, making breakfast. They had their backs to us as we came out of their tent. I was relieved to see that someone had gone to town for butane and cat food.

Harry and I tried to tiptoe past them to get to the showers. Sometimes you can tell just from the way a person scrambles an egg that he isn't in a really good mood.

"Well, the woods withstood a night of Harry," said my father. He didn't turn around, but I knew he was talking to me. "However, there is a hole in our tent, and three packages of chocolate cookes are missing from the supplies."

This was my fault too, I supposed. It was a good thing it wasn't raining. I'd be blamed for that, as well. "You know he doesn't like being left alone," I said.

My mother did turn around. She held up a

piece of paper. "I've put the tent and the cookies on your bill with the air mattress, Sara Jane," said my mother. "From now on, you'll replace everything that cat destroys from your pocket money."

Great, I thought. I'll be paying them back till I'm fifty.

"Is that clear, Sara Jane?" asked my mother.

I said that yes, that was clear.

"And do hurry, Sara Jane," said my mother. "We're almost ready to eat."

I brooded all the way to the showers, and all the way back. I was going to get even with Ben and Lucy for all the trouble they'd caused me, if it was the last thing I did. Harry, still tired from his strenuous night, woke up only when he smelled the scrambled eggs my father was serving.

"You know, there's something really wrong with that child, Mom," Lucy was saying as I sat down. "She's sickening, Mom. She really is."

Three guesses who she was talking about.

"Lucy," said my mother in her warning voice, "I'd like to get through breakfast without any arguments, thank you very much."

"Not sickening," Ben corrected. "Sick. You should hear Chicken, Mom. She really is weird. She talks to that cat like he's human or something." That cracked him up.

"He's more human than some people I know," I said coldly. I wondered what they'd say if they could hear Harry talking back, instead of the meows they did hear.

"See what I mean?" Ben spluttered. "She's sick."

"You should have heard her last night," gasped Lucy. She put on a baby voice. "'You were dreaming, Harry. Oooh, Harry, you were having a nightmare. Oooh, Harry, it's all right, let's stay here.'" This was so funny, she and Ben almost fell off their chairs.

But I wasn't going to let them upset me as they usually did. I was going to remain calm. I was going to strike when they least expected it.

"No kidding," said Ben. "You ought to get Chicken professional help. She really needs it."

"And so does that stupid cat." Lucy laughed. "He's as weird as she is. The way he meows, you'd think he was answering her."

Harry looked up from his breakfast and

hissed. He doesn't like being called stupid.

I helped myself to a cup of hot chocolate. I really hated it when Lucy and Ben ganged up on me. Life was so much easier when they fought with each other. But I didn't have any chance of that happening on this trip. Not with Harry there. They both disliked him so much that it brought them together.

Ben leaned close to me. "I wish I'd had a camera last night," he whispered. "I'd love to have a picture of you and Destructor Cat crawling out of your tent."

"If we had one of Chicken trying to drag him out of that tree, I'd have it blown up," said Lucy.

My mother frowned. "Ben! Lucy! What are you two whispering about?"

Ben tried not to laugh. "Nothing."

"Nothing." Lucy giggled.

They were getting to me. "I'm going to blow *you* up," I hissed back. "Both of you."

My mother banged her cup on the table. "Sara Jane!"

"You and what army?" sneered Lucy.

"I mean it!" my mother shouted. She looked as if she meant it. "This is the last time I'm

warning you. Because of your nonsense, your father and I hardly had a wink of sleep all night."

"But it wasn't our fault!" I protested.

"Well, it wasn't our fault, either," whined Lucy.

My mother raised her voice. "I will not spend my vacation listening to the three of you bicker," said my mother.

"What did I do?" asked Ben and Lucy together.

I stopped in midbite. "I didn't do anything," I said. Harry caught my eye. "And neither did Harry," I added.

"I mean it," said my mother. "I've come to relax, not act as referee." My mother paused. She looked at my father.

My father cleared his throat. "Your mother and I have decided that we're going to start fresh from today," said my father. "There'll be no arguments. Is that understood? We're all going to relax and have a good time."

I dropped my fork. "But I didn't start all this —"

My father held up his hand. "We're going to

forget about last night," he said. He started to eat. "I want you all to give me your word that you'll act as though last night never happened." He looked from Ben to Lucy to me. "Well? Friends from now on?"

"Okay," mumbled Ben.

"Okay," muttered Lucy.

I stared at my plate. "Okay," I said. And then I added to myself, *as soon as I get even for last night.*

The Disappearing Cat

Ben and Lucy didn't mean it when they said they'd act as if nothing had happened, any more than I did. They declared war on me and Harry.

They put a dead bird in our tent. They let spiders loose in my clothes. They stuffed our sleeping bag with leaves. They threw my sneakers into a lake. They hid Harry's food bowl. They ate the hidden package of cookies we'd been saving for a midnight snack.

They never let up for a minute. If someone farted in the car, they blamed me or Harry. If someone started snoring while my father was explaining about brass rubbings, they blamed me or Harry. If something broke, they blamed me or Harry. If something was missing, they blamed Harry or me. If Ben finished off the apples, he blamed Harry. If Lucy used up all the soap, she blamed me.

And they outnumbered me. If I tried scaring Lucy, Ben would sneak up from behind and scare me. If I tried to play a trick on Ben, Lucy would be lurking nearby to sound the alarm. And the reason they outnumbered me was that Harry refused to help.

"Your parents said to act as if that first night never happened," said Harry. "And that's what I'm going to do. Their wish is my command." Harry was ticked off because my parents never stopped complaining about him and because they called him Destructor Cat to his face. "I'm a superior life form," said Harry. "I'm not used to this sort of treatment." His sensitive feelings were hurt. "I will not stoop to your petty squabbles," said Harry. "I'm going to show your parents how perfect I really am."

"I can't believe it," said my father, with a shake of his head. "Almost two weeks gone already."

Everybody looked at him. It was dark. It was

cold. We were sitting under a tree in Dartmoor
National Park, eating our supper, exhausted
from another day of tramping through the
countryside.

"I can't believe it either," Ben muttered under
his breath. "It seems more like a year."

"Two," mumbled Lucy. "We must have seen
every old building, old tree, old grave, and old
mound of dirt between here and London."

I couldn't believe it either. I couldn't believe it
because the most interesting thing I'd done was
send Julia a postcard of a standing stone. On the
back I wrote, "Boy, do I wish you were here!"
But I also couldn't believe it because we'd been

on vacation for almost two weeks and I hadn't
come close to getting even with Ben and Lucy.
The most I'd managed was to leave Lucy's
Walkman on so the batteries died—and that was
an accident.

My father leaned back in his chair. "If you
two are going, you'd better get a move on," he
said to Ben and Lucy. "Don't forget, we have an
early start in the morning."

As a farewell to Dartmoor National Park, my
dad said Ben and Lucy could climb the nearest

hill to look for shooting stars.

"Don't go too far," warned my mother. "And be careful."

"Don't worry, Mom," said Ben. "It's just up the trail."

My father smiled at me. "Are you sure you don't want to go, too, Chicken?" he asked.

"I'm sure." I tried not to sound too happy. This was the chance I'd been waiting for. Both of them were finally going to be away from camp at the same time. At last I was going to get my revenge! I smiled at my father. "Harry and I would rather stay here," I said.

"I don't think I can take much more of this," moaned Harry. As perfect as he was, he was just as fed up with looking at old things that were falling down as the rest of us. "How many piles of stones are there in this country?"

I was busy putting things into a backpack. I didn't look up. "Lots," I said. "Millions, maybe."

"And we haven't seen them all yet?" asked Harry. "How many more can there be? Two? Three?"

I put some string, a bottle of water, a plastic

container filled with dirt, a handful of twigs, a load of rocks, and some wet newspapers into my pack. "Millions."

Harry groaned. I glanced at him. He was lying on our patched mattress with a damp washcloth draped across his forehead. Looking at piles of stone had given him a headache.

"But you were so excited before," I reminded him. "What happened?"

He gave me a look of anguish and groaned again. "What happened?" he said. "You can stand there with a straight face and ask me what happened? Chicken," Harry went on, "there's a fence around Stonehenge. There were people with video cameras at Glastonbury." He rolled over, his face in our pillow. "Everything's in ruins," he moaned. "Ruins depress me. Everywhere we go, it's all ruins." He moaned again. "Everything I remember is gone. If this is bringing the past alive, your father should have left it where it was."

To be honest, I was too busy thinking about my ingenious plan to worry much about Harry. I could hardly wait to get started. *You're a genius!* I congratulated myself. *You're an absolute genius! You don't need anybody's help, not even Harry's!* My plan was to booby-trap Ben's tent and Lucy's sleeping bag in ways they hadn't imagined. Snakes, bats, and spiders were nothing compared with what I was going to do. They'd be really sorry they'd ever frightened me and Harry.

"We'll be in Cornwall tomorrow," I said. "That's supposed to be full of history."

Harry's ears went up. "Cornwall?" asked Harry. "Chicken, did you say Cornwall?"

I picked up my pack, ready to go. "That's what my dad said."

"Where in Cornwall?"

I checked that I hadn't forgotten anything. "How do I know? I'm not the driver. I'm just a little kid."

"North Cornwall?" persisted Harry.

I peered in my pack for one last look. "Just Cornwall, Harry. What's the difference?"

"*Just* Cornwall?" Harry snapped. "What does

it *matter?*" He'd certainly gone from depressed to annoyed very quickly. "Chicken, that's like saying there's no difference between your left foot and your right."

I had everything. I was ready to go! "I'm not going to stay here arguing with you," I said. I opened the flap. I turned back to Harry. "Are you sure you don't want to help me?" I whispered. "It's going to be fun."

Harry was lying on his back, staring at the roof, deep in thought.

"Harry?"

He waved me away with one paw. "You go on and have a good time," said Harry. "I have more important things on my mind."

"Whatever you say," I said. "That's fine with me." I picked up my backpack and my flashlight, and I tiptoed into the night.

It took me almost an hour to complete my revenge. I had to be really quiet so my parents wouldn't hear me; and there was quite a lot to do. I hooked up the water so it would fall on Ben's head when he went into his tent. I fixed the twigs so they'd come down on Lucy when she closed the car door behind her. I put the dirt in Lucy's sleeping bag. I put the rocks under Ben's pillow. I stuffed the newspaper inside their pajamas.

I was so happy I wanted to sing. *You really are a genius*, I told myself as I sneaked back to our tent. *You deserve an award for this.*

I hurried inside with a cry of victory. "You should see it, Harry!" I said excitedly. "They're going to be furious! All we have to do is sit back and wait for the screams."

Harry was hunched up in the sleeping bag with the blanket pulled over his head.

"Harry," I whispered. "Harry, wake up. You don't want to miss all the fun, do you? They're going to go nuts."

Harry didn't move.

"I was afraid I might not be able to set up the water trick right," I told him as I quickly got into

my pajamas, "but I think it's going to work okay." I clapped my hands together. "I just wish I could see Ben's face when he pulls back the flap of his tent and gets soaking wet!"

Harry didn't grunt.

I gave him a shove as I climbed into bed. I switched off the flashlight. "Don't you wish you could see it, Harry?" I whispered. "After the way he scared us?"

Harry didn't budge.

"Harry." I nudged him again. "Harry, wake up. You don't want to miss this. It's going to be great. It's our moment of triumph!"

He was really depressed; he wasn't even snoring.

"Harry!" I hissed. "Come on, Harry. Stop sulking." I pulled back the sheet.

The dark makes things look weird. Harry didn't look like Harry; he looked like a bundle of clothes. I touched him. He was a bundle of clothes. I sat up. "Harry!" I shouted. "Harry, where are you?"

But there was no answer.

The cat had disappeared.

My Father Changes Direction and Harry Changes His Mind

"Harry pleaze come back chicken xxxx"

"Leave?" My voice squeaked. "You can't be serious. You'd *leave* without Harry?"

My father checked his watch. "Sara Jane," said my father, "we can't wait here all day. We should have left two hours ago." He pointed at me. "This is why we said you couldn't bring the cat in the first place." He looked across the roof of the car. "Ben!" he shouted. "Ben, hurry up!"

The whole point of the Disappearing-Cat Trick was that the cat always reappeared at the end. But not this time. I waited and waited, but Harry never came back. It was almost noon, and there was still no sign of him. And, worst of all, my family didn't care. They were willing to go on and leave poor Harry behind!

"But what if someone stole him?" I argued. "Aren't you going to wait for the ransom note?"

My father was distracted. "Ben!" he called again. "Ben, we're leaving!"

"*Stole him!*" shrieked Lucy. "Who'd steal that fat lump?" She made a face. "Even if someone was crazy enough to steal him," she continued, "there wouldn't be any ransom note. They'd pay you to take him back."

"Sara Jane," said my mother, in her reasonable voice, "we've done everything we can. We've looked everywhere. We've asked everyone to keep an eye out for him. We've left Mrs. Andreas's number with Mr. Newfield." Mr. Newfield ran the campsite. "Your father's right," my mother finished. "We can't sit here for the next two weeks. Please get in the car."

"But he might be lost. We can't just go off and leave him."

I'd hardly slept all night because I was worried about Harry. I'd been so worried, I realized, that I hadn't even heard the screams when Ben and Lucy sprung my traps.

"He has a tag," said my mother. "If he's lost he'll be returned."

"He may even have gone home," said my father. He got in the car and slammed the door shut. "Cats and dogs have been known to walk thousands of miles to get back home." He honked the horn. He leaned out of the window. "Ben!" he shouted. "Ben, let's go!"

"But what if he's hurt?" I persisted. "What if he did start to walk home and was hit by a car or something?"

Lucy rolled her eyes. "Oh, come on! Harry *walk* thousands of miles? Harry never walks farther than his supper dish."

She was really annoying me. All morning, while Mom and Dad helped me look for Harry, Lucy and Ben had done nothing but make stupid jokes about him.

"Then where is he?" I screamed. "Huh? Tell me that."

Lucy gave me this big smile. "Maybe he's gone back to Arkansas."

I'd thought of that. I'd thought that maybe Harry's spaceship had come back for him and he really had gone home. But Harry wouldn't go back to his planet without telling me first; he would never do that.

"Arcana, not Arkansas," I snapped. I wished I'd never told anyone that Harry was an extraterrestrial. It's the sort of thing that's hard to live down.

My father started the engine. "Sara," said my father. "Sara, get in." He honked the horn again. "Ben!"

I folded my arms across my chest. "No," I said. "I won't go without Harry."

"Watch out, Dad," said Lucy. "She's going to cry."

"I am not going to cry," I shouted back.

"She is, Dad," said Lucy. "She is going to cry."

"Never mind about Chicken," said my father. "What's keeping your brother?"

My mother got out of the car. "Come on, Sara," she said, putting her arms around me and leading me to the door. "If Harry turns up, Mr. Newfield will see that he gets home."

"Crybaby! Crybaby!" Lucy whispered as I climbed in. "Stick your head in cat food."

I stuck my tongue out at her.

Ben came running up. "Sorry," he panted. "I had trouble packing." He shoved his tent and his bag onto the roof.

My father leaned his head out of the window. "Make sure it's secure!" he shouted.

Ben slid in beside me and slammed the door shut. "Don't worry, Dad," said Ben. "I know what I'm doing." He poked me in the ribs. "Which is more than you can say for some of us." He laughed. "Imagine losing a cat from your own tent!"

As we drove along, Lucy listened to her

Walkman, which now had fresh batteries, my father sang along with the radio, my mother looked out the window, Ben did crossword puzzles, and I thought about Harry. I missed him. My lap felt empty without him curled up on it, sleeping. The car sounded odd without his snore. Where was he? What was he doing? Was he hungry? I looked up at the sky. It was going to rain. Harry really hates being out in the rain.

"We'll stop at the next town and get a bite to eat," said my father eventually. He glanced at my mother. "Shouldn't we be coming to Trewint soon?" he asked.

My mother looked over at him. "You mean Tintagel," said my mother.

"Tintagel?" My father laughed. "Have you been asleep, Marilyn? We're nowhere near Tintagel."

"I've heard of Tintagel," I said. "That's where King Arthur was born."

"Chicken..." My father sighed.

"In the legends," I added quickly. "Not in real life."

My mother was still looking at my father. "We just passed a sign that said Tintagel Five

Miles," said my mother.

My father shook his head. "Don't be ridiculous." He laughed. "We're nowhere near Tintagel. We're heading right for the center of Bodmin Moor."

Ben looked up from his puzzle. He tapped Lucy's knee and raised his eyebrows. Lucy pulled off her headphones. If there was going to be an argument, she didn't want to miss it.

My mother sat up a little straighter. "No, we aren't," she said very calmly. "We're on our way to Tintagel."

"Marilyn," said my father. He was trying to sound patient. "Marilyn, I am the driver. I think I should know where we're going."

"To Tintagel," repeated my mother.

"To Trewint," said my father.

Ben rolled down his window a little. "If we're heading for the moors, why can I smell the sea?" asked Ben.

He was right, you could smell the sea.

"That can't be the sea," said my father. "We're miles from the sea." He reached over and snapped off the radio. "How can I hear myself think with all that noise?" he demanded.

And that's when I heard it. It was sort of a moan and sort of a whine. It was coming from outside. "What's that?" I asked.

"I can't hear anything," said Ben and Lucy together.

"Mom," I said. "Mom, can you hear that sound?"

"It must be the wind," said my mother.

"What's that thing at the top of that cliff?"

asked Lucy.

"It's just another pile of rubble," said Ben.

"It's probably Tintagel Castle," said my mother.

The car started slowing down. "I'm going to stop and take a look at that map," said my father.

"Be my guest," said my mother, flinging the map on the dashboard.

We pulled over to the side of the road. But even though we had stopped, the sound went on. It wasn't the wind. And it wasn't a moan or a whine either. It was someone calling my name. "Chicken . . . Chicken . . . Chicken . . ." It was Harry!

"It's Harry!" I shouted.

"Have you gone insane?" asked Lucy.

"Mom! Dad!" yelled Ben. "Mom, Dad, Chicken's gone insane!"

But Mom and Dad weren't paying any attention. My father was unfolding the map very carefully, and my mother was watching him.

I unfastened my seat belt and started climbing over Lucy.

She tried to push me back. "Ow!" whined

Lucy. "Chicken, sit down!"

Ben tried to pull me back. "Sit down, Chicken," he ordered. "Can't you see we're lost?"

"We're not lost," said my father. "We're just outside of Trewint."

"You mean Tintagel," said my mother.

"Let go!" I lunged for the door.

I could hear Harry clearly once I was outside. "Chicken," Harry was calling. "Chicken, get me out of here!"

I looked around. There wasn't a cat in sight. "Harry!" I screamed. "Harry, where are you?"

"Where do you think I am?" he screamed back. "Under the hood?"

My eyes went to the luggage rack. Ben had left his bag open just enough so that Harry wouldn't suffocate. I could see the tips of his ears sticking out. "Harry!"

Ben and Lucy started giggling hysterically.

Suddenly, I understood why I hadn't heard any screams from them last night. They must have been onto me all along. While I was sneaking around, setting up my traps for them, they were laughing at me behind my back and kidnaping my cat!

By standing on the bumper, I managed to unzip Ben's bag enough to get Harry out. He threw himself around my neck. I kissed the top of his head.

Holding him tightly, I dropped back to the ground. "I'm so glad to see you, Harry," I said.

Harry leaned his head against my shoulder and purred.

It began to rain.

"I don't understand it," my father was saying. "How did we get to Tintagel? I was driving to Bodmin Moor."

I looked at Harry. He opened one yellow-green eye. "I've changed my mind about Ben and Lucy," said Harry. "I think it's time they were taught a lesson."

The Past Comes Alive

Harry was pretty upset about being kidnaped, hidden in the woods all night, and then slung on the luggage rack in a smelly old bag. He lay on the mattress in our tent, wrapped in one of my sweaters, his whiskers twitching. I put a plate of tuna and cheese in front of him. My mother let me have it to help him recover.

"Thank you," said Harry. "This has been one of the most awful experiences of my life, but I'll try to force myself to eat a little. I should keep up my strength."

He forced himself to eat the tuna, the cheese, and a bag of salt and vinegar potato chips.

"Feeling better?" I asked.

Harry stretched. "As well as can be expected," he said.

I sat down beside him. "So what are we going to do?" I asked.

Harry stuck his nose in my pocket. "You don't have any cookies, do you? I'm still feeling weak. It's the aftershock."

I took out my last piece of chocolate and handed it to him. "Don't you remember?" I asked. "You said you'd changed your mind about helping me get my revenge. What are we going to do?"

"First things first," said Harry. He licked some chocolate from around his mouth. "An army travels on its stomach, you know."

I don't know about armies, but Harry certainly does.

"That means you don't have a plan, doesn't it?" I said. I couldn't look at him. I was really disappointed. I'd been sure that Harry would come up with something really good to do to Lucy and Ben.

Harry stood up. "You don't want to rush into anything, Chicken," said Harry. "If we're going to teach Ben and Lucy a lesson, I want it to be one they never forget." His fur rippled. "Right now what I want to do is take a little walk and show you the castle." He stepped over my body and onto the ground.

"The castle?"

"Get the umbrella, and let's go," said Harry. He turned to face me and I noticed that his eyes were glowing ever so slightly. "Maybe your sister and brother would like to come, too." Harry was purring. "I'm sure they'd find it very educational."

I took a deep breath. I never liked giving

Harry bad news. "But we can't go to the castle, Harry," I said slowly.

The purring stopped. "What?"

"We can't go. My parents have grounded us for the rest of the trip. They won't let us out of their sight."

"They won't let us out of their sight?" Harry considered this for a second. His eyes darkened. "You mean they won't let us go to Tintagel?"

I shook my head. "Not without them. And my father doesn't like the idea of climbing that cliff. He doesn't think the ruins are really that interesting. He's taking us all to see the village post office instead."

"Not really interesting?" repeated Harry. He was sounding a little bit like an echo. "Your father has dragged us to every building without a roof between Wiltshire and Cornwall, and now he says that Tintagel Castle isn't interesting?" I could tell from his tone that he was almost back to his old self.

"Well, you have to admit that it doesn't look like very much from the ground," I said gently.

"I don't have to admit any such thing," said Harry. "Doesn't look like much?" He shook himself. "Trust me, Chicken, Tintagel looks like exactly what it is: the home of heroes." He raised his head. "The ancient site of heroic acts and deeds of honor. Knights lived there, Chicken. Knights and ladies. Kings and wizards. Imagine it, Chicken! Imagine what Tintagel was like a mere fourteen hundred years ago! Imagine the colors . . . the smells . . . the sights and the sounds!"

I tried to picture the ruins on the cliff top. I couldn't imagine what it was like 1,400 years ago. I wondered if Harry had a fever from riding on the luggage rack. "I thought you said you were tired of visiting ruins," I reminded him.

The whiskers over his eyes trembled. "Tintagel isn't a ruin," said Harry. "Tintagel is the birthplace of your greatest sovereign, Arthur, son of Pendragon, prince of the Silures, and king of the Britons."

"You heard my father," I said. "He says King Arthur is only a legend."

Harry sniffed. "Your father also said we were in Trewint."

"I've got it!" I pulled on my pajamas. "If we

borrow my mom's camera, we can take pictures of Ben and Lucy when they're sleeping." Ben sleeps with his arms folded under his head and his mouth open. Lucy sleeps with pipe cleaners wound up in her hair. They both look pretty dumb. "Then we can show them to all their friends when we get back home. That would embarrass them!"

Harry yawned. "You call that getting even?" he asked. "They could have killed me, and you want to take their photograph."

I climbed into the sleeping bag. "It was only a suggestion." I yanked the blanket over me. "I don't see you coming up with any great ideas." Harry had stayed in the tent all afternoon, but he still didn't have a plan.

"You're a very impatient little girl, Chicken," said Harry. He stretched out beside me. "Camelot wasn't built in a day, you know."

"I thought that was Rome," I said. I rolled over and closed my eyes. "Rome wasn't built in a day."

Harry started purring. "In this case, Camelot, I think," he said.

It was the sound of horses that woke me up.

The horses were just outside our tent. I could hear them stomping and whinnying. I pulled the blanket over my head and turned over.

The horses started laughing and talking.

"Harry," I mumbled. "Harry, tell the horses to be quiet. They'll wake up my parents."

One of the horses started singing a song.

I turned over again. "Harry," I hissed. "My father will go mental if singing horses wake him up in the middle of the night. Go and tell them to be quiet."

Something hard hit the roof, just above my head. I sat up. I opened my eyes. A strange light was glowing through the walls of the tent.

"Harry!" I whispered. "Harry, is it morning already?"

Harry didn't answer.

"Harry!" I called, feeling for him in the dark. "Stop fooling around!"

Something else hit the roof of my tent. Men were shouting and laughing. I might have thought it was Ben and Lucy again, but even if Ben and Lucy could sound like horses, I was pretty sure they couldn't smell like horses.

"Harry! Harry, where are you?" I didn't really need to ask. Harry always disappears when you need him most. Just like his spaceship. It must be an Arcanan trait.

The sounds outside seemed to be fading away. As quickly as I could, I put on my slippers and crept to the front of the tent. I pulled back the flap and peered out.

It wasn't night any longer. It was a bright, sunny day. But it wasn't a bright, sunny day at our campsite. The campsite was gone, too. My parents' tent, Ben's tent, and our car were all gone as well.

I looked around. There was no sign of the shouting men or of the smelly horses, but there were two arrows sticking out of the roof of my tent. As I crouched in the entrance, staring up at the arrows, my tent disappeared too.

"Harry!" I yelled. "Harry, you come back here!"

I got to my feet. I was standing on one side of a grassy meadow. The meadow was dotted with wildflowers and surrounded by deep woods. There were no planes in the air and no traffic on the road. In fact, there was no road. And then, just at the edge of the forest, I saw a cloud of dust.

"What is this?" gasped Lucy. "What's going on?"

The sound of her voice right beside me made me jump. Somehow, I'd completely forgotten about her and Ben. I glanced over my shoulder, wondering if my parents were going to turn

up, too.

"It's a dream," said Ben. He was standing on the other side of Lucy. "We're having a dream."

Lucy frowned. "All of us?"

"Yeah," said Ben. "It's a group dream."

The cloud of dust was moving toward us. "Actually," I said, "I think it may be horses."

I was half right. It was horses; but on the horses were knights. The knights wore armor and carried shields and long, painted lances.

The three of us just stood there gaping as they approached.

"This is incredible," said Lucy.

"It's only a dream," Ben repeated.

"I wish I knew where Harry was," I said.

Halfway across the field, the knights came to a sudden stop. There were twelve of them in a row — twelve knights, each wearing a white tunic bearing his coat of arms. "Ben! Lucy!" The twelve knights were laughing. "Now it's our turn for a little fun!"

"This isn't a dream," said Lucy. "It's a nightmare." She turned to Ben and then to me. "But why are we all having the same one?" she demanded.

I didn't know what to say. When you live with a visitor from another planet, you get used to having strange things happen now and then. But this was the first time that time and space had gone a little weird when Ben and Lucy were around.

The knights raised their shields. "You like games!" they called. "Well, let the games begin!"

With a nod and a shout, the knights began to move forward again, slowly at first. Lucy grabbed my hand as the horses picked up speed. "They're going to run us over!" she cried. "They're going to trample us to the ground!"

She did have a point. They seemed to be heading straight for us. But I couldn't react. How often do you get to stand in a field with a bunch of knights in shining armor? Real knights? In real armor? All I could think of was that they were really there. *Knights*, I kept saying to myself, *real live knights!* Talk about bringing the past alive!

Lucy squeezed my hand. "Help!" she screamed. "Help! Help!"

"Run!" shouted Ben. He tugged on my arm.

The cloud of dust thundered toward us.

I closed my eyes.

When I opened them again, Ben and Lucy had vanished. I was standing in the courtyard of a large castle. The castle was made of gray stone and hung with banners. *It's a castle!* I thought to myself. *A real castle!* Soldiers stood guard on the battlements; flags fluttered from the towers. I couldn't believe my eyes. Other people went to the seaside on their vacations, but here I was at a real castle! I took a deep breath and almost fell

over. I don't know what I'd thought castles smelled like, but this one smelled a little like a forest and a lot like a stable.

I started to walk around, hoping I might run into Harry. There were hundreds of people all jammed together in the courtyard. They were dressed in everything from velvet to rags, but I was the only one in striped pajamas. I wished I'd worn my bathrobe.

Some were on horseback and some were on foot, but I was the only one in hippopotamus slippers. I hoped nobody would look down.

Not that I really needed to worry. Everyone was very busy. There were people pulling carts and leading mules or cows. There were people carrying chickens and pigs. One man was pushing a goat from behind. One man was dancing with a large brown bear. Six dwarfs, dressed in red, were doing acrobatics. Minstrels, jugglers, and vendors selling pies and desserts strolled through the crowd. Everyone was talking, shouting, and laughing at once. I'd never seen anything quite like it before. Not even when my parents took us to a theme park. I didn't know which way to look first.

And then a group of people near me began to clap. I stood on tiptoe to see why they were applauding. There was some sort of playing field right in front of me, but I couldn't get a clear view. *Cricket?* I wondered. *Soccer? Hockey?* I almost wished my father were with me. He'd know when soccer was first played in Britain.

The crowd began to cheer wildly. I jumped up and down, trying to see, but all I could catch were glimpses of open space.

"May I assist you, Sara Jane?" asked a deep, quiet voice above me.

I looked up. Standing beside me was a tall, thin man. He was dressed all in black, except for a single silver earring in the shape of a crescent moon. He wore his hair in one long braid, and his eyes were as sharp and bright as stars. For some reason, it didn't seem odd that he knew my name. Before I could answer, he reached down and lifted me onto his shoulders. I decided it was probably just as well my father wasn't with me, after all.

What a view! Not only could I see the field and the stands filled with onlookers, but I could see the castle behind them, and the sea behind that. I could see for miles. I felt as though I were sitting in the sky.

The crowd cheered again.

The twelve knights entered the field and began circling it on their horses. It wasn't a soccer game. I definitely wasn't about to see a game of cricket, or hockey, or even rugby. The first two knights rode into the center, the others all came to a halt in the farthest corner. What I

was about to see was a jousting tournament! A real joust! I clapped my hands together. Oh, how I wished Harry were with me. He loved spectator sports.

"Pay attention, Sara Jane," said my new friend.

"I am paying attention," I replied — and that was when I saw them. Seated behind the first two knights were Ben and Lucy. The knights were laughing. Lucy and Ben, however, were not laughing. They weren't even smiling just a little. They were scowling and looking through the crowd. Somehow, I knew that they were looking for me.

Lucy spotted me first. "Chicken!" she screamed. "Chicken! Get us down from here!"

Ben joined in. "Chicken!" he yelled. "Chicken, do something!"

Do something? What did they expect me to do? I wasn't even dressed.

People were pointing at Ben and Lucy and laughing. They did look pretty funny in their

pajamas, riding on chargers with knights. Lucy even had her pipe cleaners in her hair.

"Sara Jane Thomas!" Lucy screamed. "This isn't funny! This is all your fault, and you know it! Get us down from here this minute!"

"You just wait, Chicken!" yelled Ben. "You're going to be sorry for this!"

The first two knights turned their horses and

faced each other across the field. They pulled down their visors.

I thought it was possible that I would be sorry for this. If my parents ever found out. I just knew they wouldn't understand about jousts.

A trumpet sounded. The crowd began to cheer again. "Long live Arthur!" they roared. "Long live Pendragon!"

Arthur? *King* Arthur? But I couldn't worry about that. I decided it was time I helped my sister and brother. Just in case. I didn't want my parents to appear suddenly, screaming at me, even if it was just a dream.

"Let me down!" I shouted. Nothing happened. I leaned forward so I could see his face. "Please," I begged, "you have to let me down. Ben and Lucy —"

Those starlike eyes stared into mine. The man in black pointed straight ahead. "*Shhh*," he commanded. "It's the king."

I looked. A small, dark man was just stepping onto the platform opposite us. He was dressed in purple and gold. On his head was a jeweled crown. In his right hand he held a large sword. The handle of the sword was covered with

jewels as well. He raised it in greeting. It flashed
like lightning. All I could do was stare.
"To the finest knights in
Christendom!" shouted
the king.

The knights leaned forward. They lowered their lances.

"Let the games begin!" ordered the king.

The two knights — and Ben and Lucy — began to charge.

The crowd went wild.

Ben and Lucy went wild.

"Sara Jane!" they screamed. "Sara Jane! Do something! Quick!"

But I couldn't even look at Ben and Lucy. I couldn't look at them because I was looking at someone else. Not the king, but at the man who had suddenly appeared beside him. He was tall and thin, and all in black, except for a silver moon that dangled from his ear. He wore his hair in one long braid, and his eyes shone like stars. He was staring right at me, and I was staring back. I looked down. I was on the same man's shoulders. Somehow I knew that if the king was Arthur, then the man beside him must be Merlin. And the man on whose shoulders I was sitting must be Merlin too. I looked back across the field. The other Merlin was holding something in his arms.

It can't be, I told myself. I leaned forward. It was. The man beside the king was holding a large gray cat. The cat was asleep.

"Harry!" I shouted. "Harry, wake up! Harry, help me!"

The knights raced past each other, their lances cracking against the metal of their armor. My sister and brother shrieked. The crowd cheered.

But the cat didn't stir. The Merlin standing beside the king winked at me.

"Harry!" I yelled. "Harry, do something!" I tried to get down, but two strong hands held me tight.

"Harry! Harry, you have to help!"

"Don't make such a racket, Chicken," grumbled Harry. He stretched out across my chest and yawned. "You know I like to be woken up gently."

I rubbed my eyes and looked around. We were in our tent, still in our sleeping bag. It was morning. Outside, I could hear the birds chirping and my parents starting breakfast.

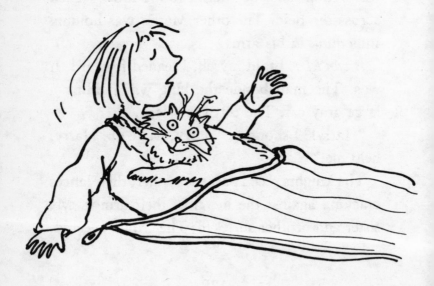

Over my head, I could see the outline of a branch that must have fallen on our roof in the night.

"Harry," I said, "you won't believe the dream I had."

Harry yawned again. "Tell me after breakfast," he said.

A Vacation Never to Forget

Ben and Lucy brought Harry breakfast in bed. There were scrambled eggs, bacon, toast with jam, and fried tomato. Harry loves fried tomato almost as much as he loves cheese.

"We wanted him to know that we're really, really sorry for yesterday," said Lucy.

I was too surprised to answer. Something wasn't right. Ben and Lucy always apologize when they do something to me or Harry because my parents make them. This was different, though. This time they really seemed to be sorry.

Harry, who had gone back to sleep while I was trying to tell him my dream, opened one eye.

Ben put Harry's bowl down beside the air mattress. "What Lucy said goes for me, too," said Ben. He patted Harry's head. "I'll never do anything like that again. I promise."

Harry opened both eyes and rolled toward the edge of the bed, sniffing.

"That's what you say now," I replied. "But by tomorrow you'll be picking on us just as you always do."

Lucy shook her head. "No, we won't, Chicken, really." She turned to Ben. "We've learned our lesson, haven't we?"

Ben nodded. "That's right, Chicken. We've learned our lesson. We'll never do anything to scare you or Harry again."

Harry was sort of dripping off the mattress in the direction of the food. He scooped up some egg with his paw.

I sat beside Harry, studying my brother and sister. Yesterday they could hardly stop laughing long enough to apologize. Today they were treating Harry like a king. Something was fishy. "How come?" I asked.

Lucy widened her eyes. "How come what?"

"How come you're being so nice? How come

you've learned your lesson? You'd never learned your lesson before."

Ben looked at Lucy. Lucy looked at Ben.

"No special reason," said Ben.

"We just realized how bad we acted, that's all," said Lucy.

"What? While you were sleeping?" I can be sarcastic when I want to be.

Ben looked at Lucy. Lucy looked at Ben.

That's when I knew. They didn't think I was being sarcastic. They thought I was asking a question.

"What makes you say that?" Ben demanded. He sounded nervous.

Lucy gave me a thoughtful look. "Sara Jane Thomas," she said, "have you been eavesdropping on us?"

I decided to let her think what she wanted. I smiled. "I just wondered if you could remember what it felt like riding in a tournament," I said.

"What a dream!" Ben grinned. "It was so real. At first I was really scared, but when I think about it now, it was the most fun I've ever had."

Lucy was still giving me her thoughtful look. "How do you know so much about our dream?"

she asked.

I glanced over at Harry. He was busy licking the jam off a piece of toast and didn't look up.

"Me?" I said. "I don't know so much. What could I know?"

Ben and Lucy made such a fuss about spending more time at Tintagel that my parents decided we'd stay where we were for a few more days. "Well, as long as you're so interested," said my father, "of course we'll stay."

Harry and I went for a walk after breakfast. When we came back, my father and Ben had the map spread out on the folding table.

"There are supposed to be some very interesting ruins around here," my father was saying, jabbing at the map with his finger.

"Great," said Ben. "Maybe after we've climbed to the castle, we could stop in the village." Ben and Lucy had even convinced my father to take us up the cliff. "I'd like to buy a book about the history of the area," said Ben. "You know, find out a little more about it."

My father couldn't have looked more surprised if Ben had said he wanted to windsurf on the moors, but all he said was, "That's a terrific idea."

Lucy was sitting in a beach chair, reading my mother's guidebook. She looked up. "I want to find out all I can too," she said and sighed. "Just imagine what it must have been like to live hundreds and hundreds of years ago. Imagine if you were a beautiful lady, and a handsome knight went into battle for you." She smiled at my father, who was staring back at her in amazement. "It really makes you think, doesn't it?"

My mother looked at my dad. "Well what do you know," she said. "It looks as if this vacation's working after all." She looked at me. "What about you, Chicken? Have you become interested in the past, too?"

I sat down, gently moving Harry from leaning against my shoulder to lying in my lap. He curled his tail around himself and went right back to sleep.

"Oh, yes," I said. "I think I have."

Harry wouldn't tell me how he'd done it. How he'd made us all have the same dream. He said I must be confusing him with someone else, he

-136-

wasn't a magician, he was an extraterrestrial. I mentioned Merlin and he gave me a look. "I don't know what you're talking about, Chicken," he said. "Hasn't your father told you

that Merlin and Arthur are only legends?"

While Harry dozed, and my mother and sister read, and Ben and my dad planned what we'd do for the next few days, I sat and thought. Ben, Lucy, and I had had the same dream. A dream about knights on horseback and a jousting tournament. A dream about King Arthur and Merlin. A dream so real that Ben and Lucy had changed. I stared into the distance. On the other side of an old stone wall there was a large field. There was something familiar about this field. The grass was high and dotted with wildflowers. The woods were gone, but there were still a few trees huddled together at the farthest end.

It was a very unusual dream, I said to myself.

My mother suddenly put down the book. "You know what?" she said. "I think that maybe this really *will* be a vacation we never forget."

"Well, I know I'm never going to forget it," said Lucy.

"Me neither," said Ben.

I stared hard at the clump of trees at the end of the field. I almost thought there was something glinting in the shadows, like sunlight on metal.

If it was a dream, I thought.
Harry started purring.

THE END

Don't miss these other
Harry and Chicken adventures:
Harry and Chicken
Harry the Explorer

C#2
Sheldon, Dyan   Backup J
   Harry On Vacation   Fic

	DATE DUE	